The Soft-Hearted Sheepdog

Harvey rested his head on his outstretched paws again. Let's face it, he thought as he closed his eyes. No one's going to want a failed sheepdog – no matter what Denzil says.

"Look, Dad! It's a lovely Border Collie."

Harvey opened one eye to see a little girl looking straight at him.

He opened his other eye.

"He's beautiful," said the girl.

SYLVIA GREEN

The Soft-Hearted Sheepdog

Illustrated by Peter Kavanagh

SCHOLASTIC INC.

New York Toronto London Auckland Sydney
Mexico City New Delhi Hong Kong Buenos Aires

For Don
S.G.

For Debbie and Tony,
with love from Pete

ISBN 0-439-62569-6

12 11 10 9 8 7 6 5 4 3 2 1   3 4 5 6 7 8/0

Printed in the U.S.A.   40

First Scholastic printing, November 2003

Chapter 1

Sunnyside Dogs' Home

Harvey was a sheepdog with a problem. He was terrified of sheep.

Now the farmer who owned him had taken him to a dogs' home. He was a kind man – but he couldn't afford to keep a dog that didn't work.

Harvey shook his long black and white coat and lay down in his run. His sad brown eyes moved around, taking in his new surroundings. Sunnyside Dogs' Home didn't look very sunny to him.

"Hello there."

Harvey turned to see a dog in the next run. At least he assumed it was a dog. It looked like just a mass of long, brown matted fur with a longer furry mass that wagged at the other end.

The creature shook itself and a lot of bits flew off it. Then Harvey could just make out two small black eyes peering through the tangled mass.

"Just arrived, have you?" A pink tongue emerged now.

"Y-yes." Harvey stood up. "My name's Harvey."

"I'm Denzil," said the furry mass. "You're a sheepdog, aren't you?"

"Well, not exactly," said Harvey. He didn't want to admit to being afraid of sheep. He'd wanted to work. He'd tried. He'd really tried. But there was something about sheep… He shuddered at the thought of them.

"I am a Border Collie," he told the furry mass. "But I – er – don't really like sheep."

"Don't blame you," said Denzil. "Silly creatures. Always following each other."

Harvey liked him immediately.

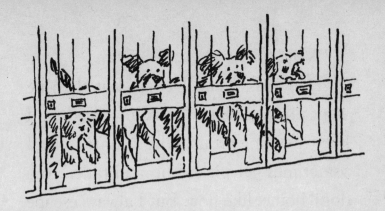

All of a sudden the other dogs started barking like mad. Harvey could see them jumping up all along the line of wire runs.

"What's happening?"

"Don't ask," said Denzil. Then he added: "It's just someone come to choose a dog. The dogs always go mad – they all want to be picked."

"Don't you want to be picked?" asked Harvey.

"No one's going to want me." Denzil snapped at a small crowd of flies that had gathered above him. "Anyway, I don't want to be chosen."

"Why?"

"Don't ask," said Denzil. But then he went on to explain: "I like my freedom. I like travelling around the country. Oh, I sometimes get picked up and taken to a dogs' home, like now. But I always escape again – after a couple of good meals." He settled down for a scratch.

"I'd rather like to be taken to a nice new home," said Harvey.

"Well, there shouldn't be a problem for you," said Denzil. "You're young, good-looking." He peered at him through his matted fur. "All you gotta do is perfect the soulful eyes."

"Soulful eyes?"

"Yeah. You look up at 'em with big soulful eyes – then they can't resist you. Works every time."

Harvey was just going to ask more when Susan, the kennel maid, arrived with some food. Denzil attacked his as though he hadn't eaten for a week. But then maybe he hadn't.

Harvey wasn't hungry. He lay down with his head resting on his front paws.

"You gotta eat." Denzil looked up from his bowl, bits of food sticking to the long fur on his chin. "You gotta keep fit and healthy. Folks won't pick a half-starved looking dog."

Harvey still didn't move. Everything was so strange.

"Look, if it will help, I won't escape until you've been taken to a new home," Denzil offered. "I'll stay with you, keep an eye on you."

It would help. Denzil was so kind. Harvey managed to eat a little of his food and then had a nap. But he didn't rest. He dreamed about the first time he'd been put in a field with a flock of sheep.

He'd really wanted to do well. And he knew what to do. But as he got closer to the sheep they looked bigger and bigger. And woollier and woollier! And their staring faces looked scarier and scarier!

Harvey froze! His heart pounded in his chest. His owner had whistled to him but Harvey couldn't move. Then one of the sheep took a step towards him.

Harvey turned tail and fled right out of the field.

A phobia, the vet had said it was. No real reason for it – it was just like some humans were afraid of spiders. Harvey felt a complete failure.

He woke up to see Susan going into Denzil's run. She swatted at the crowd of flies above him. "It's a bath for you, my boy."

"Here we go again," he said to Harvey. "They always imagine I'm going to look different when I've had a bath. But I always look the same."

Susan led the way out of the run.
Denzil followed her. The flies followed
Denzil.

Almost immediately all the dogs
started barking and jumping up at the
wire again. Someone else was obviously
coming to choose a dog.

Harvey rested his head on his
outstretched paws again. Let's face it, he
thought as he closed his eyes. No one's
going to want a failed sheepdog – no
matter what Denzil says.

"Look, Dad!
It's a lovely
Border Collie."

Harvey opened one eye to
see a little girl looking
straight at him.

He opened his
other eye.

"He's beautiful,"
said the girl.

Beautiful? Harvey lifted his head. This little girl liked him. And she had a kind face. What was it Denzil had said about eyes? Big soulful eyes. That was it – can't resist you, he'd said.

Harvey sat up and made his eyes as big as he could. He wasn't sure if they were soulful as well, but big would have to do.

"I don't know, Beth," said Dad. "He doesn't look very lively to me."

Harvey was on his feet in seconds. Dad wanted a lively dog. He could be lively. He ran to the wire and jumped up, wagging his long black tail with the white tip.

Beth laughed. "He's showing you he can be lively."

This girl understood him. Harvey was hopeful. He began to chase his tail round and round.

Beth came into the run and Harvey bounded over to her. She stroked his long black and white fur.

"This is definitely the one I want," she said. She rubbed Harvey's silky ears gently and looked into his brown eyes. "Would you like to come and live with us?"

Harvey was sure that he would. He put a paw up to touch Beth's knee.

She laughed. "Please, Dad. You did say that I could choose."

Chapter 2

The Strangest Looking Creatures

Harvey sat beside Beth on the long seat in the truck with his head on her lap. He snuggled in. She was nice and soft.

His one regret was that he hadn't been able to say goodbye to Denzil. He really hoped he could meet him again one day.

"Here we are," said Beth, as they pulled into a driveway. "You'll like it here, Harvey. We've got a nice big farm for you to run around in."

Farm? She'd said farm. That probably meant sheep. Yikes! Harvey shrank back as Dad opened the door to get him out.

"Come on, boy," said Dad. "What's the matter?"

"Perhaps it's because I mentioned farm," said Beth. "He might think we've got sheep. You know, they told us about his problem at the home."

"Come on, Beth. He can't really understand what you say."

"Collies are very intelligent dogs," said Beth.

Harvey raised one eyebrow. Of course he was intelligent. He just didn't like sheep. And of course he could understand what Beth said. Just because he couldn't talk human…

Beth bent her face close to his. "It's all right, Harvey. We haven't got any sheep. And there aren't any sheep anywhere near here."

That was all right then. Harvey immediately sat up and licked her face. Then he jumped down from the truck and stood wagging his tail as he waited for her.

"See?" Beth laughed.

"Coincidence," said Dad.

Harvey looked around him. He thought he might like it here. Then Beth took him into the house and gave him a biscuit. Not a dry old dog biscuit but a real human-type chocolate digestive. That clinched it. He definitely liked it here.

Dad said that he had to go and check on his newly-sown field of winter wheat.

"We'll come with you," said Beth. "Come on, Harvey."

They set off over the fields. Harvey soon started to worry about Dad and Beth. Dad kept hanging back to look at things and sometimes Beth ran ahead. What were they doing? They should keep together.

He ran backwards and forwards urging them to stay together. Then he kept behind them, running with his head kept low, in a zigzag pattern.

Beth laughed. "What's he doing?"

"He's rounding us up," said Dad. "He might be afraid of sheep, but he's got the natural herding instinct that collies have." He bent down to fondle Harvey's ears. "Poor old boy. You're a bit of a mix-up, aren't you?"

Harvey wasn't sure that he wanted to be a mix-up.

Apparently the winter wheat was okay when they got to the field – all Harvey could see was just a few spiky bits sticking out of the ground. But Dad seemed happy with it.

Back at the farmyard, Harvey spotted the ducks waddling all over the yard. He quickly rounded them up and sent them, quacking in protest, back into the pond.

"Harvey," Dad shouted. "Leave the ducks alone."

But – but… He'd only been trying to help. Of course, he couldn't make Dad understand that.

Dad was talking to Beth now. "I know we got him as a pet," he was saying. "But he's really a working dog. We could have trouble with him."

Trouble? Harvey didn't want to cause trouble.

"But we haven't got any work for him to do," said Beth. "We haven't got any – you know – S.H.E.E.P. And anyway he's frightened of them."

"I know," said Dad. "But he's not acting like a normal pet dog. We'll have to see how he goes."

"Oh, Dad, he's only ten months old," said Beth. "He'll soon settle down." She bent to stroke Harvey's silky ears.

Good old Beth, thought Harvey. He gazed up at her with his big brown eyes and tried to look soulful.

Beth gave Harvey a big bowl of Meaty

Chunks for his dinner. Beth and Dad had meaty chunks too but they had potatoes and peas with theirs so it took them longer to eat it. Harvey was allowed to go outside while they finished.

He chased his tail for a while. Then he chased some autumn leaves that had fallen. He raced around, his long black and white fur blowing in the breeze.

"And who are you?"

Harvey skidded to a halt to see a large tabby cat sitting in the last patch of evening sunshine.

He eagerly bounded over to meet her. "Hello. I'm Harvey."

The cat didn't offer her name but sat looking at him while she washed her right ear with her paw. "What do you do here?" she asked.

"Do? Well, I live here."

"I'd worked that one out," she said haughtily. "But *why* are you here?"

"Oh, that's easy." Harvey wagged his long black tail with the white tip. "I'm here because Beth loves me. She picked me—"

"She loves me too," the cat interrupted. "In fact, she absolutely adores me. But I've still got a job. I'm useful."

"What do you do?" Harvey sat down to listen.

The cat made him wait while she washed the end of her long tail. Then she suddenly looked up, her green eyes flashing. "I catch mice and rats."

Harvey was very glad he wasn't a mouse or a rat.

"I guard Dad's wheat and corn for him. Otherwise the mice and rats would eat it all." She lifted a paw to inspect it and flashed her claws. "And I'm very good at it."

"I–I'm sure you are."

"I'm teaching my kittens to hunt too. They want to be useful."

As if on cue, three tabby and three black and white kittens scampered out of the barn. They danced round their mother a few times then began chasing each other all over the yard.

Harvey jumped up. He'd show this snooty cat that he could be useful too. He chased after the kittens to round them up for her.

Immediately, the cat sprang after him. Harvey stopped as she appeared in front of him. Her back was arched and her fur stood on end. "Don't you dare chase my kittens," she spat.

"Harvey. Leave the cats alone." It was Dad's voice.

"But…" If only he could tell him he was trying to help again.

The cat immediately ran up to Dad and began rubbing herself against his legs. Her green eyes softened as she gazed adoringly up at him.

"It's all right, Sheeba," said Dad, bending to make a fuss of her. "Who's my good girl, then?" He turned to Harvey. "She's the best mouser in the county, we have to take good care of her."

Huh, thought Harvey. I should think that's one cat that can take pretty good care of herself.

He trotted off to explore more of his new territory. He hadn't made a very good start with Dad. He didn't know how Dad wanted him to behave. He'd never been a pet dog before.

Dad obviously loved Sheeba because she was useful to him. Harvey wanted to be useful too.

Suddenly, he heard some strange noises and raced round the corner to investigate.

"Yikes!" He skidded to a halt at a wire fence. He was faced with some of the strangest looking creatures he had ever seen.

Chapter 3

A Working Dog

"What, what, what?" The creatures all looked up as Harvey appeared.

There must have been five hundred of them. Their long necks bobbed up and down and bright red pieces of knobbly skin flapped about under sharp-looking beaks. They eyed Harvey with small, bright, beady eyes. "What, what, what?"

Then they all lifted their heads and stretched their necks. "Gobble, gobble, gobble, gobble, gobble." The noise was incredible.

What on earth were they? Harvey sat fascinated, ears pricked and head on one side.

They quietened down but still eyed him suspiciously. Some had white feathers and others were a bronze color. But they all had strange knobbly red heads. They strutted around on large feet and twittered to each other all the time.

Dad appeared round the corner. He chuckled as he saw the puzzled look on the dog's face. "They're turkeys, Harvey. I guess you've never seen any before."

Harvey definitely hadn't. He tilted his head the other way. They still looked peculiar – whichever way you looked at them.

"I've got to put the turkeys away now," Dad told him. "You can wait here if you like but you'll have to sit still and be very good. I don't want you frightening them. They're very nervous creatures."

Harvey sat very still and watched, his tongue lolling out, as Dad pushed open a gate in the wire fencing.

The turkeys started to run all over the place as Dad walked amongst them. "What, what, what? Look out, out, out."

Harvey dropped his head to one side and watched intently as Dad held out his arms and started shooing the turkeys towards a hut on the other side of the run.

"What, what, what? Help, help, help!" they shrieked and ran this way and that.

Eventually several were inside, but as Dad went to get the others some of the first ones came out again.

Dad stopped and wiped his forehead. "Stupid creatures, it's the same every night," he muttered under his breath.

Harvey's eyes were bright. He was straining to sit still as he'd been told.

He gave an eager little whine. He could help. But he didn't want to upset Dad again.

His head jerked from side to side as he watched the large, ungainly birds running about in confusion.

He looked at the gate. It wasn't fastened. But Dad—

He couldn't sit there any longer. One leap at the gate and he was inside, amongst the turkeys. They shrieked and fluttered in panic.

"Harvey!" Dad shouted.

But Harvey ignored him – he had to prove himself to Dad. He crouched low and, keeping his belly to the ground, began to slink round the outside of the flock.

The turkeys watched him with their beady eyes as they backed away.

Harvey moved swiftly round them, his tongue lolling from his eager, open mouth. He began driving them towards the open door of the hut.

When one or two broke away from the group, Harvey raced after them and expertly drove them back. He raced backwards and forwards, driving them with just enough pressure to keep them moving, but not too much to frighten them.

Dad watched in silent amazement.

The turkeys were still twittering to each other but no longer in a panic.

Then the largest bronze male turned on Harvey. He raised his tail feathers and fluffed his body feathers out to make himself look bigger. He eyed the black and white dog defiantly and refused to budge.

Harvey fixed him with his eye. He stared at him, holding the turkey spellbound by the strength of his gaze.

His confidence seemed to calm the bird and it turned and joined the flock again.

Harvey expertly drove the whole flock into the hut. Dad came and closed the door behind them.

"Well," he said to Harvey. "You have just achieved in a matter of minutes something it usually takes me an hour to do."

Harvey's eyes were bright as he sat at Dad's feet and looked up at him. Dad wasn't cross with him this time. He'd actually done something right.

"Good dog, Harvey. Well done," said Dad, patting his head. Then he set off towards the house. Harvey immediately trotted just to the left of him, keeping to heel. Dad looked down at him and smiled. "You even managed to sort out Big Tom. That's the big turkey that tried to give you trouble," Dad explained. "All the male turkeys are called Toms – or Stags. But I always call that one Big Tom. He gives me more trouble than any of them."

He laughed. "Hark at me, I'm talking to you as though you understand everything I say – just like Beth thinks you do."

Beth came out to meet them. She smiled at the sight of Harvey at the heel of his new master. "You're back early tonight," she said to Dad.

"It's thanks to this young pup here," he said, looking down into Harvey's soft brown eyes. "Wonderfully intelligent dog. You should see him round up turkeys. We really made a good choice when we chose him."

"Yes, *we* did, didn't *we*," said Beth.

Harvey licked her hand.

Chapter 4

Danger!

Harvey was so proud. He had his very own herd.

All right, so it was turkeys instead of sheep. But it was his herd, his responsibility.

He went every morning with Dad to let the turkeys out. They usually came out of the hut on their own, but he liked to see they were all right.

He checked on them regularly during the day, while Dad was out in the fields with his tractor. Then every evening he rounded the turkeys up and drove them into their hut for the night.

Dad had been right – he was a working dog, and now he had some work to do. He was useful.

And both Beth and Dad loved him.

Sheeba wasn't impressed with his new job. But Harvey wasn't really surprised. She didn't seem to be interested in anything that didn't involve catching mice or rats.

Beth often had to go to somewhere called school, and Harvey eagerly raced to greet her when she returned. They went for walks together and played games with a ball or a stick. In the cold evenings Harvey sat beside the fire with his head on Beth's knee. She stroked him and talked to him. Sometimes she gave him a cookie. At night, he slept at the foot of her bed.

He was happy and contented. He often wondered about Denzil, his friend who had been so kind to him at the dogs' home. Was he somewhere warm or was he outside, travelling the roads again?

One night, a couple of weeks later, Harvey woke up feeling uneasy. Something was wrong. He jumped up, waking Beth.

"What's the matter, Harvey?" she asked sleepily.

Harvey didn't know what was up. Was it a sound that had woken him, or was it just instinct? He ran downstairs and Beth followed in her dressing-gown and slippers.

"Do you want to go out?" she asked, opening the front door.

Outside, Harvey sniffed the air. His keen sense of smell picked out a strange smell – a different smell. A smell of danger mixed with fear. He barked loudly to warn Beth.

"I'll get Dad," said Beth.

Harvey raced off into the darkness. He heard the turkeys' terrified shrieks before he reached the run.

"Help, help, help! Look out, out, out! Help, help, help!"

The hut was still all closed up. What could be happening?

"Yikes!" He spotted a hole dug under the wire fence. "Fox!"

Now he knew what the smell was.

He opened the gate by pushing the latch up with his nose and sped across the run.

A broken plank of wood that had been wrenched aside showed Harvey that the fox had got into the turkeys' hut. He might have killed some already!

He desperately tried to get through the hole. It was too small.

He raced round to the door just as Beth and Dad arrived. Dad was in his pajamas and still looked sleepy as he opened the door and switched on the light.

All Harvey could see was feathers flying everywhere. The turkeys shrieked and flapped in the air.

Then he spotted it. A flash of red-brown fur.

"A fox!" cried Dad, seeing it too. "He could very quickly kill several of the smaller turkeys. The rest are likely to injure themselves in their panic!"

Harvey moved swiftly. He had to separate the turkeys from the fox. He forced his way through the chaos, dodging fleeing turkeys and ducking under flying feet.

"Move!" he barked to the turkeys. He urged as many as he could outside whilst keeping an eye on the whereabouts of the fox.

The fox spotted Harvey. It backed into a corner but Harvey could clearly see its white front on its red-brown body. Its sharp black nose and its keen eyes glinted in the electric light.

Dad and Beth went outside to keep an eye on the turkeys. There were still quite a few left inside but now there was more room for them to escape. And there was more room for Harvey to deal with the fox!

The fox was smaller than Harvey and it cowered in the corner. White and bronze feathers still rained down on them as Harvey moved slowly towards it, growling deep in his throat. He stared hard at this intruder that had dared to threaten his herd.

The remaining turkeys were all watching, huddled together, their heads bobbing.

Suddenly, the fox made a run for it. It shot behind the turkeys.

"Gobble, gobble, gobble, gobble, gobble," they cried. Feathers and straw flew again as they ran in all directions. "Help, help, help. Look out, out, out."

Harvey made a run at the fox, scattering the turkeys to all sides. "Get out!" he snapped. He bared his teeth and growled threateningly.

The fox bared his sharp pointed teeth at Harvey. But Harvey was in no mood to be threatened. He leapt forward and bit the fox on the nose.

That was enough for the fox. With a yelp it shot out of the hut door and back through the hole under the fence.

Beth rushed into the hut and flung her arms round Harvey's neck. "Oh, you clever dog," she cried.

"Yes, well done, Harvey," said Dad. "I'd have lost a lot of turkeys tonight if it hadn't been for you."

Harvey felt so proud. He quickly rounded up the turkeys that were outside while Dad filled in the hole under the wire and nailed a fresh piece of wood to the hut.

On quick inspection none of the turkeys seemed to be hurt. Their terrified shrieks gradually turned into a low twittering. They all eyed Harvey, their heads bobbing. Did they realize he had saved them? Were they actually grateful?

It was then that he realized how fond he had become of them. Such funny, nervous creatures. And they needed him.

The next morning the turkeys came rushing out of their hut, led by Big Tom. They actually looked pleased to see Harvey. It gave him a lovely warm feeling.

Harvey saw Beth off to school and then Dad decided to go into town to buy some more wire and wood to stop the fox getting in again. Harvey was allowed to go with him and sat proudly up on the passenger seat of the truck.

Dad parked in one of the wide streets. "You'll have to wait here, Harvey," he told him. "Dogs aren't allowed inside."

Harvey looked happily around him as he waited for Dad. The building across the road looked familiar.

"Sunnyside Dogs' Home!" He sat upright. "I wonder if Denzil's still there?" There was no sign of Dad coming back yet – and he'd left the window open. Harvey jumped out and crossed the road.

He quickly found a small gap in the hedge and squeezed through. No one was about so he ran over to the wire runs.

He saw him almost straight away. "Denzil."

The familiar furry mass looked up and shook himself. He'd been right, he didn't look any different after his bath. "Harvey," he cried. "What are you doing back here?"

"I've come to see you," said Harvey. "I'm glad you're still here. But how come you haven't escaped yet?"

"Don't ask," said Denzil. Then as usual he went on to answer anyway. "Actually the food's pretty good here and the people are nice – I dunno – perhaps I'm getting old. But I'm planning to be on my way again soon."

Harvey told him where he lived now and all about Beth and Dad. Then he told him about his job looking after the turkeys. "I'm really busy," he told Denzil. "The turkeys need a lot of looking after."

"Oh well, you won't be so busy soon," said Denzil.

"Why?" Harvey was puzzled.

"It'll soon be Christmas," said Denzil.

"Christmas? Why should that make any difference to my job?"

"You mean you don't know?"

Harvey shook his head.

"Well," Denzil took a deep breath.

"The traditional Christmas dinner is –
well, it's turkey."

"Turkey?" Harvey's ears went back.

"You mean they…" He couldn't bring himself to finish.

Denzil shook his head slowly. "I'm sorry, Harvey, but what you're actually looking after is five hundred Christmas dinners."

"Oh, no!" Harvey couldn't bear the thought.

"Turkeys aren't pets," Denzil

explained. "Farmers, like Dad, raise them to sell at Christmas."

"No," said Harvey. "Well, maybe that's what's going to happen to other turkeys – but not my herd. I'll get them away. Hide them."

Denzil had a quick scratch. "Where on earth could you hide five hundred turkeys?"

"I don't know," said Harvey. "I'll think of something. Just tell me, how do I know when it's Christmas?"

"There are signs," said Denzil. "One of the first things the humans do is bring a tree indoors."

"A tree?"

"Yes, then they hang things on it, shiny things usually – and they hang things around the house too. Then there's the baking."

"Baking?"

"You'll smell that," said Denzil. "Spicy Christmas puddings, mince pies and sausage rolls – oh and a special cake… Look out. There's someone coming."

"I'd better go," said Harvey.

"Good luck," called Denzil.

Harvey raced away before he was caught and squeezed back through the gap in the hedge. He had just jumped into the truck when Dad came out.

Dad swung rolls of wire and planks of wood into the back of the truck and climbed in beside Harvey. He rubbed his head fondly. "Good boy. I wasn't long, was I?"

Harvey gazed up at him. He loved Dad. But he loved the turkeys too – and they trusted him. He had to save them.

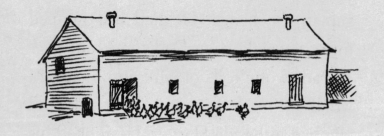

Chapter 5

The Perfect Place

The next morning, when the turkeys all tumbled out of their hut looking so pleased to see him again, Harvey knew he'd made the right decision. He had to find somewhere safe to hide the turkeys until after Christmas.

He searched all morning, all around the fields and hedgerows but he couldn't find anywhere that would be suitable.

"Oh, dear," sighed Harvey. "It's not going to be easy finding somewhere to hide five hundred noisy, nervous birds."

He popped back at lunchtime to check the turkeys. Beth hadn't gone to school today so he made a quick dash into the kitchen to see if she was baking. She was – but it was only an apple pie. Harvey had seen them before and they definitely weren't on Denzil's Christmas list.

Beth made a fuss of him with her floury hands, making Harvey's coat more white than black. She laughed as she tried to brush it off. Harvey would have loved to have stayed and played with her, but he had work to do.

He did a quick tour of the house and was relieved to see no tree had been brought in yet.

In the afternoon he searched around the churchyard and all along the riverbank. But nowhere was suitable.

He went back for his dinner and checked the turkeys again. There were no strange baking smells in the house and the trees were all still in the orchard.

"Will it be an apple tree or a plum tree they bring in?" Harvey wondered. "It seems a very strange thing to do."

Sheeba was waiting for him by the turkey run. "Where've you been all day?" she demanded.

"Nowhere," said Harvey, although his legs felt like he'd been *every*where. But he wasn't going to tell her anything.

"It's not like you to leave your precious turkeys for so long," she taunted.

Harvey ignored her.

Sheeba licked her lips and looked at Harvey with a wicked gleam in her green eyes. "I'm really looking forward to my Christmas dinner."

So she knew too. Well she wasn't going to get her teeth into any of his turkeys.

Harvey was more determined than ever to save them.

The next morning he went way beyond Dad's fields, past the church and past the river.

Suddenly, he found himself in an open grassy area he had never been to before. The wind blew his fur as he raced around. There wasn't a building or a person in sight. He scrambled down a grassy slope into a valley.

At the bottom was a broken, overgrown railway line.

He ran along the line to an old railway tunnel. It was blocked off at the far end and had bushes growing in front of it. They would provide shelter from the wind at night.

There was plenty of greenery for the turkeys to eat in the daytime and grit on the railway line for them to peck at. There was even a hollow with water in.

"This is it," said Harvey. "The perfect place to hide the turkeys until after Christmas."

He raced back to the farm. Sheeba was waiting again. "Where have you been to this time?" she demanded. This cat didn't miss a trick.

Harvey was feeling pleased with himself. "It's none of your business," he told her. He held his head high and marched straight past. That showed her. All he had to do now was keep a watch out for signs of Christmas.

The next morning everything still looked normal in the house. Harvey checked on the turkeys and counted the trees in the orchard. They were all still there.

He heard Beth calling him from the house. She probably had a cookie for him – or wanted to play a game. Harvey raced indoors and straight into a heap of paper and cardboard on the floor.

This was a good game. He leapt about in the heap with bits and pieces all over him.

Beth giggled. "Oh, Harvey."

Harvey tossed a small, star-shaped piece of cardboard off his head. He looked at it as it fell to the ground. It was shiny. He leapt round to look at the other bits and pieces. They were all colourful – and shiny.

Were these the shiny things Denzil had told him about?

He heard a noise in the doorway and turned to see Dad staggering through with a tree. Not one from the orchard, but a different one he hadn't seen before.

"There, Harvey," said Beth. "I wanted you to see the Christmas tree."

Harvey felt himself stiffen. Christmas tree! Then these were the shiny bits to put on it. This was it then!

Beth was showing him the star. "It goes on the top of the tree," she explained. "And that's tinsel you've got in your tail. Isn't it pretty?"

Dad put the tree down and laughed. "You look a bit like a Christmas tree yourself, Harvey."

Harvey shook the bits off him. He had to get the turkeys away.

Tonight.

Chapter 6

Escape!

Harvey waited until both Beth and Dad were asleep. Then he crept downstairs, past the brightly decorated Christmas tree, past the spicy smelling puddings and pies that were cooling in the kitchen.

He lifted the latch on the back door with his nose and padded out into the night. He was going to miss Beth and Dad. But it wouldn't be for long. He'd bring the turkeys back straight after Christmas.

"What are you doing out at this time of night?"

"Yikes!" Harvey's heart leapt as Sheeba sprang out in front of him.

The nosy cat had guessed he was up to something.

He'd have to think quickly. Get rid of her.

"Wow, look at that enormous rat," he cried. "It's just run into the barn."

"What rat?" Sheeba eyed him suspiciously.

"Of course, it was much too big for you," said Harvey. "But Dad will understand."

"What do you mean?"

"When he sees how big the holes in the sacks of corn are," said Harvey. "He'll realize the rat was too big for you to catch."

That did it. With a defiant swish of her tail, Sheeba turned and headed for the barn, calling for her kittens to come and help her.

Harvey chuckled to himself. That would keep her busy for the rest of the night. She wouldn't give up now.

He quickly reached the turkey run and pushed the latch on the gate up with his nose. He raced to open the door of the hut.

The turkeys were all fast asleep.

"Wake up," he called.

Immediate panic set in. "What, what, what?" they cried.

"Shh, shh, it's only me," said Harvey gently. "We've got to leave."

"What, what, what? Why, why, why? Look out, out, out."

Harvey glanced out of the door. He could just see the outline of the house in the distance. The lights were still out – Beth and Dad hadn't woken.

"Trust me," said Harvey urgently. "We've got to leave. You're in danger here."

"But it's late, late, late."

He realized it was no good talking to them. He'd have to be firm. He rushed past them to the back of the hut. "Out. Now. All of you."

The turkeys flapped and gobbled and complained but one by one they jumped out of the hut. They ran in all directions.

Harvey dashed backwards and forwards, crouching, springing, and urging. It took all his skills but he finally managed to get them through the gateway and then over to the lane.

They turned the wrong way down the lane.

"Yikes!" Harvey raced ahead of them to turn them. He had to get them off the lane as quickly as possible. There shouldn't be anyone in the lane at this time of night, but he couldn't take any chances. Harvey kept them moving with just enough pressure to keep them going, but not too much to spook them. They strutted down the lane in front of him, heads bobbing and turning, twittering and grumbling to themselves.

Then Harvey raced to the front of the herd and turned them into a field on the other side.

An owl hooted and frightened them. They ran in all directions all over the field. Harvey raced after them to round them up again. It was very different from rounding them up in the confines of their run. And in spite of the moonlight it wasn't easy to see them all in the dark. The white ones showed up all right but the bronze ones were difficult to see. If only he had some help.

He managed to herd them all across the field to a gap in the stone wall on the other side. Big Tom turned on him, his feathers ruffled in defiance.

"You've got to go through that gap," Harvey told him.

"What, what, what? Why, why, why?"

The large turkey stared at him, his beady black eyes glinting in the moonlight.

Harvey held him with his eye. "We've got to cross the field on the other side. Trust me. If you go through first the others will see there's nothing to be afraid of."

Big Tom still stared at him. Then he gave two bobs of his head, three gobbles and, with a sudden flap of his wings, fluttered through the gap.

Harvey rushed round the rest of the flock. "Right, now the rest of you. Through you go," he barked.

The rest of the flock complained, squawked and fluttered their way through the wall.

Harvey leapt through after them. He rounded them up again and urged the flock forward. He ran behind them in a zigzag pattern to keep them in check. As soon as he spotted any stragglers he immediately sprang forward to round them up again.

They crossed the field and Harvey managed to get them all through the open gateway and into the next field.

It had recently been ploughed and the turkeys complained as they fluttered and stumbled over the deep furrows. Harvey raced backwards and forwards to keep them moving, leaping lightly over the rough ground.

The next field was grass again but still the turkeys complained. "Can't we stop, stop, stop? We're tired, tired, tired."

"I'm tired too," said Harvey. "But we must go on."

He kept them moving, past the field of winter wheat, past the churchyard.

It took every skill he could muster, driving, blocking, and turning the reluctant birds. It was difficult, keeping them on course on his own.

The journey was taking much longer than Harvey had realized. He had to get the turkeys to their hiding place before daylight. Out in the open fields they could easily be spotted. It wasn't exactly an everyday sight to see five hundred turkeys and a dog travelling across the fields on their own. Someone would be bound to inquire where they had come from.

Harvey herded them across the field that went down to the river. The gate on the other side was shut. Harvey pushed the catch up with his nose to let the turkeys through on to the riverbank. The catch slid up over the post, but the gate didn't swing open.

Then he spotted the padlock! He wouldn't be able to open this gate.

"Now what am I going to do?" he said. "I don't think there's another way round."

The turkeys were all twittering and looking up at him, their heads bobbing. One thousand black, beady eyes glinted in the moonlight.

"You could all jump over the gate," he said to them. "But by the time you're all over, the first ones will probably have run off and fallen in the river."

Suddenly he heard a noise behind him.

The turkeys heard it too. "What, what, what? Help, help, help." They fluttered off in all directions.

Chapter 7

Don't Ask!

"Denzil!" Harvey couldn't believe his eyes. There was his old friend standing in the field with his mouth crammed full of feathers. "What are you doing here?"

Denzil spat the feathers out on to the ground. "Don't ask." He looked round at the turkeys, now scattered to all sides of the field. "I thought you might need a hand."

"I certainly do," Harvey chuckled. "But how'd you get here? How did you find us?"

"I escaped from the home and went to the farm. Then," Denzil nodded towards the pile of feathers on the grass, "I followed your trail. You'd left a trail of feathers all the way here."

"And you've gathered them all up," said Harvey. "Oh, Denzil. I'm so pleased to see you."

Denzil looked around him. "Okay, now what? You'd better give the orders. I'm not sure I'm cut out to be a sheepdog – or should I say turkey-dog."

Harvey got Denzil to jump the gate and wait on the other side to stop the turkeys running into the river. Then, with quite a bit of encouragement from him, one by one they all flapped and squawked their way over the gate.

Harvey herded the turkeys along the riverbank. Now, with Denzil helping, it was so much easier.

They crossed a couple more fields and reached the railway tunnel just as it was starting to get light.

The turkeys complained as Harvey drove them down the steep sides of the railway embankment. "What, what,

what? Oh dear, dear, dear. Look out, out, out."

"This is your new home," said Harvey. "For a little while anyway."

Their shrieks and complaints echoed round the tunnel as Harvey drove them in.

"They're not very grateful, are they?" said Denzil. "Did you tell them why you'd brought them here?"

"Oh, no," said Harvey. "I couldn't tell them *that*. It'd be far too upsetting for them."

Denzil shook his head. "You're a softie."

Harvey and Denzil lay down across the entrance to the tunnel. Inside, they could hear the turkeys shuffling around to get comfortable.

"What about food?" Denzil whispered.

"There's plenty of green stuff for the turkeys to eat here," Harvey told him. "And they like scratching around for worms and insects. They usually have turkey pellets as well but I'm sure they can manage without for a while."

"What about you?" Denzil asked, sitting up.

"I didn't think about me," said Harvey. "I'll find something."

"We can catch mice, rats, that sort of thing," said Denzil.

"Oh, I couldn't kill anything," said Harvey. He had a sudden vision of Sheeba, with her sharp claws and teeth.

"I was right, you *are* a softie," said Denzil. He lay down again with a big sigh. "But then if you weren't, we wouldn't be here now, saving five hundred turkeys from Christmas."

They all slept well into the morning.

Then the first few turkeys woke up. "What, what, what?" they cried, craning their necks and looking around them. That woke the rest of them up. They all stretched their heads and necks. "Gobble, gobble, gobble, gobble, gobble."

Denzil sat up. "What a row! Are they always like this?"

Harvey chuckled. "Always."

Some of the turkeys were strutting towards the entrance of the tunnel. Big Tom pushed his way to the front of the group. He eyed Harvey with his black beady eyes.

"It's okay," Harvey told him. "You'll be all right here."

Big Tom tossed his head, shaking his bright red skin flaps, then he led the way out. The turkeys all strutted past Harvey and

Denzil, twittering amongst themselves.

They marched along the railway line, heads bobbing and peering round them all the time. Some ventured up the sides of the banking to investigate. Then they all raised their heads. "Gobble, gobble, gobble, gobble, gobble."

Denzil cringed.

Harvey ran after them and picked a spot high up on the banking to lie down and keep watch.

Denzil joined him. Together they watched the turkeys pecking and scratching at the grass. Some had found a bed of nettles halfway up the slope and were enjoying a good meal. Others were pecking at the grit around the railway lines. Big Tom was enjoying a dust bath between the sleepers.

Denzil shook the long tangled fur from his eyes and studied them. "Strange looking creatures. Haven't got a lot of common sense. And you certainly can't have a good conversation with them.

How come you got so fond of them?"

"I don't know, really." Harvey rested his head on his front paws but his eyes were alert, watching all the time. "I know they complain a lot but that's just their nature. They do seem to like me. And they trust me. I just couldn't let them be – you know what."

Denzil nodded. Then he rolled over. "You gonna lie here all day?"

"I've got to keep a watch on them." Harvey didn't move but his eyes still swivelled over his flock.

"I'll go and find us some food," said

Denzil, getting up. "I'm starving."

As soon as Denzil left, Harvey had to leap up and bring back two of the turkeys that had climbed too high up the banking. He had just laid down again when four more took off along the railway line. Harvey raced after them and brought them back to the main herd.

Then he sat watching, tongue lolling out of his open mouth, the wind blowing his long fur.

Eventually, Denzil appeared over the top of the banking. He had something trailing from his mouth. The turkeys all shrieked as he dragged a long string of sausages down the slope.

Harvey laughed. "Where on earth did you get those?"

"Don't ask," said Denzil. This time he didn't go on to explain.

Harvey wasn't sure he wanted to know anyway. The two dogs dug into the sausages, one starting at each end of the string. When finally they met in the middle they were both full up.

The rest of the afternoon passed peacefully enough. As soon as it began to get dark, Harvey started herding the turkeys into the railway tunnel. They were complaining as usual, their shrieks of protest echoing round the large tunnel.

Suddenly Harvey's keen ears picked up another sound. "There's someone coming," he told Denzil.

"You get the rest of the turkeys inside and I'll go and see," Denzil offered.

Harvey had just got them all inside when Denzil returned. "It's a man and a little girl," he told him. "They're definitely looking for something. And they're heading this way."

"It must be Dad and Beth," Harvey breathed.

"You've got to keep this lot quiet," said Denzil. "They'll be here any minute."

Harvey's heart was thudding in his chest. "Quiet," he hissed to the turkeys. "You've got to be quiet."

"Why, why, why?" cried the turkeys. "We're fed up, up, up. Boss, boss, boss."

"You must," said Harvey. "Please. Just for a while."

"Fed up, up, up," the turkeys repeated. "Boss, boss, boss. Why, why, why?"

Denzil stepped in amongst them. "I'll tell you why. 'Cos if you don't be quiet – you're all gonna die!"

Silence.

Not a gobble – not a twitter.

Harvey breathed a sigh of relief. He hadn't wanted the turkeys to know the truth – but it had worked.

He could hear voices above them. The man and girl must be on top of the railway tunnel.

Inside, all was quiet in the darkness.

Harvey could only hear the occasional harsh breath and the muffled shuffling of one thousand large scaly feet.

"They couldn't have got this far." It was Beth's voice. "And we've looked everywhere else."

"If they've escaped they'd have scattered everywhere," said Dad. "They're too stupid and panicky to stay together. We'd have seen at least one or two of them."

"The whole flock's been stolen," said Beth. She started to cry. "And Harvey's gone too."

Harvey couldn't hear what else they were saying as they were moving away. Were they blaming him? Were they cross with him? He hadn't stopped to think how Dad and Beth might feel about it.

Chapter 8

Christmas

Panic gripped Harvey. Perhaps Dad and Beth wouldn't want him back now.

He thought of Beth with her kind face, her soft lap – her cookies. He suddenly realized how much he missed Beth – he missed her much more than her cookies. And Dad. He thought of how he smiled at him when he'd done well.

He shivered in the entrance to the tunnel. Denzil and the turkeys didn't seem to feel the cold. But he was used to being beside the fire in the evenings with his head on Beth's knee. He'd never sit there again if they wouldn't have him back. Perhaps he should take the turkeys back now...

He glanced into the tunnel where the moonlight picked out the sleeping shapes of some of the turkeys. Big Tom opened his eyes. He looked at Harvey with such trust and – affection – Harvey was sure he wasn't imagining it. No, he couldn't take them back. Whatever happened to him he wouldn't take them back until after Christmas. When exactly would that be? He glanced at Denzil who was snoring beside him. He'd know.

The turkeys were much better behaved after Denzil had warned them of their fate. They still complained, but that would never change.

Every morning Harvey let the turkeys out to scratch and feed on the green slopes of the railway cutting while he kept watch on them. In the evenings he rounded them up to spend the night in the tunnel.

Big Tom always stayed quite close to Harvey now and gradually the others stopped wandering off so far. They were still wary of Denzil, but they seemed to like being near Harvey.

Denzil kept the two dogs well supplied with food. Sometimes it was bits of meat, sometimes more sausages and sometimes pieces of leftover hamburgers or other tasty morsels. He never let on where he got any of it.

It was getting colder and several days had passed when Harvey woke to see a strange sight.

"What's happened?" He reached out a paw to touch the white stuff that had covered everything in the night. It was cold. Very cold, but fluffy. He tried sniffing it. The soft, cold flakes went up his nose and made him sneeze.

Denzil opened one eye and chuckled. "It's snow," he told him.

"What's snow?"

Before he could answer, a strange ringing echoed round them. Harvey put his head on one side to listen.

"Church bells," Denzil explained. "It must be Christmas day."

"It is?" Harvey felt a surge of excitement. "We've made it! We've saved the turkeys!"

"Yep. And it's a white Christmas by the look of it," said Denzil.

Harvey ventured out into the snow. It came halfway up his legs, but once he got used to the cold, it was fun. Harvey leapt and turned and tossed the snow with his nose.

Some of the turkeys ventured out. "What, what, what?" they cried, as their feet disappeared into the snow. They scratched and pecked at the strange white substance. "Gobble, gobble, gobble, gobble, gobble." That brought the rest of them out of the tunnel.

Harvey watched them strutting about, lifting their feet high. Their heads bobbed and turned as they looked around them. "What, what, what? Tut, tut, tut." They all glared at Harvey.

Harvey laughed. "It's not my fault. I didn't put it there."

Five hundred pairs of feet soon flattened quite a wide area outside the tunnel and the turkeys set about scratching to find something to eat.

Harvey shook his long coat to remove the melted snowflakes. "D'you think it will be safe to go home tomorrow?"

Denzil nodded. "Any time after Christmas day."

"Let's go tonight then," Harvey decided. "Get the turkeys back first thing tomorrow—" He stopped suddenly, remembering his fears. "Supposing Dad and Beth are so cross with me they won't have me back?"

"There's only one thing you can do," said Denzil.

"Look up at them with soulful eyes?" asked Harvey.

"Soulful eyes aren't enough here," said Denzil. "You've gotta be sneaky."

"Sneaky?"

"It's the only way," said Denzil. He stood up and shook himself. "We'll take the turkeys back but you stay away for a couple of days."

"Stay away? Why?" Harvey was longing to be home with Dad and Beth. Beth with her kind face, her soft lap and her—

"Because," Denzil interrupted his thoughts, "if you're not there when the turkeys get back, Dad and Beth won't know it was anything to do with you, will they?"

"No – I suppose not."

"You just arrive a couple of days later and they'll be real pleased to see you," said Denzil.

"You are clever," said Harvey.

Denzil grinned beneath his long tangled fur. "And sneaky."

Chapter 9

Homeward Bound

They set off at dusk. Harvey wanted to make sure they got the turkeys back before Dad and Beth were up. They always got up as soon as it was light.

It started to snow again. The turkeys were already complaining, as they wanted to go to sleep. This cold stuff falling on them as well was just too much.

They raised their heads in common protest: "Gobble, gobble, gob—" They stopped as the snow fell into their open beaks.

Denzil laughed. "Now perhaps we'll get some peace for a change."

It took ages getting the turkeys up the railway banking in the snow. They slipped and slid all over the place.

When they eventually reached the top Harvey looked over his herd. "One's missing," he said.

Denzil looked at him in amazement. "How can you tell? They all look the same. And there's five hundred of them."

"I know them all," Harvey insisted. "And one is missing." He slithered back down the snowy bank. There was no sign of the missing bird. Harvey raced around and his expert nose soon picked up the scent he was searching for. He began to dig furiously at the snow.

"What, what, what?" A frightened but somewhat annoyed turkey emerged from a heap of snow and shook itself. It had obviously fallen down the banking into a deep pile of snow.

Harvey quickly ushered the turkey up the banking. Several more had wandered off.

"I tried to stop them," said Denzil. "But I'm no good at this sort of thing – at least not on my own."

Harvey rounded them up again and urged them forward. They'd lost quite a bit of time. They had to get back before it was light if Denzil's plan was to work.

It was very dark now and there was no moon – only the snow gave off its mysterious light. On the way to the railway tunnel it had been easier to pick out the white turkeys in the darkness. Now, against the snow, only the bronze ones stood out.

Harvey barked orders to Denzil and between them they managed to keep the flock together and moving. The turkeys kept their heads down against the falling snow and muttered their complaints.

The snow slowed them down quite a lot and when they reached the ploughed field, several turkeys fell down the ruts. Harvey dug them out while Denzil watched the rest of the flock.

The journey took so long that it was getting light when they reached the farm.

"What are we going to do?" said Harvey. "Dad and Beth will be up."

"We can't take the turkeys all the way back now," said Denzil.

Harvey looked around him. "There's no one about yet. Maybe I can get them away quickly." He looked at the turkey run. The gate was open – that was a start – he could drive them straight in. "If I can just keep them quiet…"

He moved the flock forward. "You mustn't make a sound," he warned them. "You'll soon be in your own dry home again."

They were all amazingly quiet as they obediently filed into their run. Even the hut door was ajar. It was going better than he'd dared hope.

The first turkeys went into their hut. Harvey sighed with relief. In only a couple of days he could come back. He longed to see Dad and Beth. But he had to wait—

"Help, help, help!"

The quiet was suddenly shattered. A terrific shrieking and fluttering arose from inside the hut. The turkeys still outside immediately joined in the general panic. "What, what, what? Look out,

out, out. Gobble, gobble, gobble, gobble, gobble."

Then several dark shapes shot past Harvey.

"Sheeba. And her kittens." They had been inside the hut!

The turkeys shrieked and rushed in all directions as the cats ran amongst them.

The seven cats, in fear of being trampled on, howled at the stampeding turkeys.

Denzil barked as several turkeys streaked back out of the gate.

"Quiet! For goodness' sake be quiet!" Harvey hissed at them all.

Not surprisingly, no one could hear him.

"What's going on?"

Yikes! It was Dad's voice. He was coming.

"It can't be – it's the turkeys!" Beth was coming too.

It had all gone wrong. Now they'd know it was him that had taken the turkeys.

"Quick! Let's go," Denzil called from the gate.

Harvey looked round him. Neither Beth nor Dad had reached them yet. He crouched low and, keeping his belly to the ground, slid round the other side of the turkeys in the run.

He made the gate.

"Come on," said Denzil.

Harvey's heart was pounding as he raced after Denzil towards the lane.

"How? Why?" Dad was shouting. He must have reached the run now.

The two dogs skidded into the lane.

Harvey stopped. Several of the turkeys had fled back to the lane in their panic. He couldn't leave them. They'd get lost. Dad would never find them on his own.

If he kept low, he could just get them back…

Harvey silently sped round and managed to get them off the lane. He urged them forward in the direction of their run. "Just keep moving," he hissed. "I've got to go."

"Harvey!" Beth had spotted him.

It was all over. He'd be sent away. Back to the dogs' home.

Harvey had never felt so miserable in his life.

Beth rushed at him and flung her arms round him. He'd been caught.

To his surprise she buried her face in his long fur. "Oh, Harvey." He could feel her hot tears on his cold neck. Why was she crying? Was it because she knew Dad would send him away now?

"Dad," she called. "Harvey's here as well."

Dad rushed out of the turkey run.

"Harvey? Good heavens! So that's how they got back." He ruffled his coat and patted him. "You good, clever dog."

Good? Clever? Harvey didn't understand what was going on.

"We were so upset when the turkeys were all stolen," Beth told him. "And we thought you'd been stolen too."

"Or run away," said Dad. "But all the time you were out looking for them."

"And you found them," said Beth, stroking him fondly.

It slowly began to dawn on Harvey what they were talking about. They believed that thieves had stolen all the turkeys and that Harvey had been out looking for them – and brought them back.

He couldn't tell them the truth even if he wanted to.

"They're all here," said Dad, looking round him. "Every one of them."

Harvey felt a pang of guilt – but it didn't last long. After all, everyone was happy now – especially him. He jumped up at Beth and then Dad, wagging his tail and licking them wherever he could reach.

"Dad," said Beth. "You won't kill the turkeys now, will you?"

"No," said Dad. "Nobody wants five hundred turkeys *after* Christmas."

"But what about – you know – next Christmas?"

Harvey held his breath.

Big Tom gulped and opened his beak.

"They'll be too old by then," said Dad. "They'll be…" He broke into a whisper. "Tough."

Harvey let out his breath.

Big Tom closed his beak.

"You know, I didn't realize I would miss them," Dad laughed. "It's shown me I haven't really got the heart to be a turkey farmer. I think this first try will be my last. I'll stick to farming the land from now on."

"Can we just keep the turkeys then?" asked Beth.

"Oh, I don't know," said Dad. "There's five hundred of them. They cost a lot to feed."

Harvey looked up at Beth, his big brown eyes willing her to think of something.

"Eggs!" she cried.

"Eggs? They're not chickens," said Dad.

"I know," said Beth. "But turkeys lay eggs too, don't they? Only the other day a lady was here asking about them. She said she used to enjoy a good turkey egg when she was younger."

"Well, that's a thought." Dad rubbed his chin. "They'll be ready to lay come February. Nice big eggs they lay too."

"We can sell them," said Beth. "And the turkeys won't be any trouble with Harvey to look after them."

Harvey wagged his tail to show his agreement.

"All right," said Dad. "Who knows – perhaps we'll start a new trend. Everyone will be wanting turkey eggs."

Harvey was so excited. The turkeys had survived this Christmas and they hadn't got to worry about next Christmas – or any Christmas from now on. He rushed over to Big Tom and licked his knobbly face.

The turkey looked a bit surprised – and wet. Then he stretched his head and neck. "Gobble, gobble, gobble, gobble, gobble."

The rest of the herd joined in and Dad and Beth laughed.

Harvey suddenly remembered Denzil. He was waiting for him in the lane.

He raced back to him. But wise old Denzil had guessed that Harvey was being allowed to stay. He was already walking down the lane.

"Wait," called Harvey. "I'm sure they'll let you stay too."

"I'm too old to change my ways now," said Denzil, looking back. "But don't worry, I'll be popping back from time to time to see what you're up to."

"Harvey!" Beth was calling him.

Harvey still looked after Denzil. "But where will you go?"

"Don't ask," said Denzil. "Now you get back there, where you belong."

Harvey wagged his long black tail with the white tip. Then he raced back to Beth and Dad – and to his very own herd.

The End